Far from Home

A Story of Loss, Refuge, and Hope

Sarah Parker Rubio

illustrated by Fátima Anaya

TYNDALE KIDS

Tyndale House Publishers, Inc.
Carol Stream, Illinois

Library of Congress Cataloging-in-Publication Data
Names: Rubio, Sarah Parker, author.
Title: Far from home : a story of loss, refuge, and hope / Sarah Parker Rubio.
Description: Carol Stream, Illinois : Tyndale House Publishers, Inc., [2019]
   | Summary: "A small boy has to leave his home suddenly, leaving his
   extended family and most of his possessions behind. In the middle of a
   very trying journey, a kind stranger tells the boy the story of Jesus'
   escape to Egypt"-- Provided by publisher.
Identifiers: LCCN 2018037066 | ISBN 9781496436733 (hc)
Subjects: LCSH: Jesus Christ--Flight into Egypt--Fiction. | CYAC:
   Refugees--Fiction. | Loss (Psychology)--Fiction. | Parent and
   child--Fiction.
Classification: LCC PZ7.1.R82763 Far 2019 | DDC [E]--dc23 LC record available at https://lccn.loc.gov/2018037066

For Mamá—Thank you for making it home,
wherever we were.

This used to be my room.

My bed was right here, with my blanket and my pillow and Rabbit.

I was sleeping here in my bed when I woke up in the middle of the night and heard grown-ups talking.

"We need to go to a new country," they said. "It's not safe here anymore."

"Wake up," Daddy said. "We have something to tell you."

I pretended I was still sleeping.

"I know you're awake," Mama said. I can never fool her.

I opened one eye. Mama and Daddy tried to smile.

"I don't think I want to hear what you're going to say," I said.

I was right.

"We have to leave home," Daddy said.

"For how long?" I asked.

"A long time," Mama said. "Maybe forever."

"Are Grandma and Grandpa and all my friends coming?" I asked.

"Not now," Daddy said. "Maybe later."

Mama and Daddy tried to tell me why, but nothing they said made any sense.

These used to be my toys.

Cars and planes and my helicopter.

Elephant and Lion and Bear—and, of course, Rabbit.

"You can only take one toy," Mama said. "Choose your favorite."

They were all my favorites.

I chose Rabbit, because I'd had him the longest.

9

"We have to go right now," Mama said. "Hurry!"

I hurried so fast I almost forgot Rabbit.

We walked for a long time. Then we got on a bus. Then we walked some more.

"It's an adventure!" Daddy said.

I didn't want an adventure. I wanted to go home.

"Don't worry," Daddy said. "Soon we'll be in a new country. You'll have a new room and new toys and new friends."

I wanted my old room. I wanted my old toys. I wanted my old friends.

After the buses and the walking, there was waiting. And then more waiting. And then even more waiting.

"Why did we have to hurry if we're just going to wait?" I said.

"Please don't whine," Mama said.

So I zipped my mouth up tight and shoved all the whining down into my tummy, even though it made my tummy hurt.

But the whining didn't want to stay down. It got bigger and bigger, until it was so big I couldn't keep it down anymore.

"NO MORE WAITING!!!"

Then everyone looked at me.

There was nowhere to hide, so I just hid my face in Rabbit's tummy.

13

Somebody touched me on the shoulder. I didn't want to take my face out of Rabbit's tummy, but the somebody kept touching my shoulder, so finally I did.

14

The somebody was an old lady. Her face had millions of wrinkles. But she was smiling so big that even her wrinkles looked happy.

15

"Do you want to hear a story?" the old lady asked.

I didn't want a story. I wanted to go home. But Mama was watching. So I said, "Yes, please."

"Good!" the old lady said. "This is one of my favorite stories. A long, long time ago, there was a little boy like you."

"Did he have a Rabbit?" I asked.

"I don't know," the old lady said. "If he did, it probably wasn't as nice as yours."

I thought that was probably true.

"The little boy was sleeping in his bed when suddenly his mama woke him up."

I held Rabbit tight. Mamas waking you up in the middle of the night is bad news.

19

"The boy's mama said they had to leave their home. For a long time. Maybe forever. His mama and daddy tried to tell him why, but nothing they said made any sense.

"The boy had to leave most of his toys. He and his mama and daddy had to wait for a long time.

"Finally the boy got to his new home. But it was strange. His room was different. The food was different. The people were different."

21

"What happened to the boy?" I asked.

The old lady smiled. "He learned how to live in a new place. And another new place after that. He grew up and helped many people. He could heal people when medicine didn't work. He could feed a crowd with one person's food. He saved a lot of people's lives."

She put her hand on my shoulder again. "But he never forgot what it was like—the leaving and the waiting and the different."

23

I leaned back against Mama and hugged Rabbit tight. Mama stroked my hair.

"Is that story true?" I asked the old lady.

The old lady smiled her biggest smile yet. "Oh, yes," she said.
"It's one of the truest stories in the world."

25

This is my room now.

My new bed is right here, with my new blanket and pillow. Same old Rabbit.

The food here is different. The weather is different. The people are different.

But I think I will find new friends here.

Sometimes I miss my old home. But when I feel sad, I remember the story the old lady told me.

And I remember that I am not alone.

An angel of the Lord appeared to Joseph in a dream. "Get up! Flee to Egypt with the child [Jesus] and his mother," the angel said. "Stay there until I tell you to return, because Herod is going to search for the child to kill him." That night Joseph left for Egypt with the child and Mary, his mother.

Matthew 2:13-14

Sarah Parker Rubio edits children's and young adult books by day and writes them by night. She was born in the United States, grew up in Costa Rica and Ecuador, and now has a bilingual and bicultural family with her husband, Colombian composer Gary Rubio. They live in the Chicago area with their two sons, Gabriel and Adan; two sassy cats, Perry and Bono; and a giant white dog named Finn.

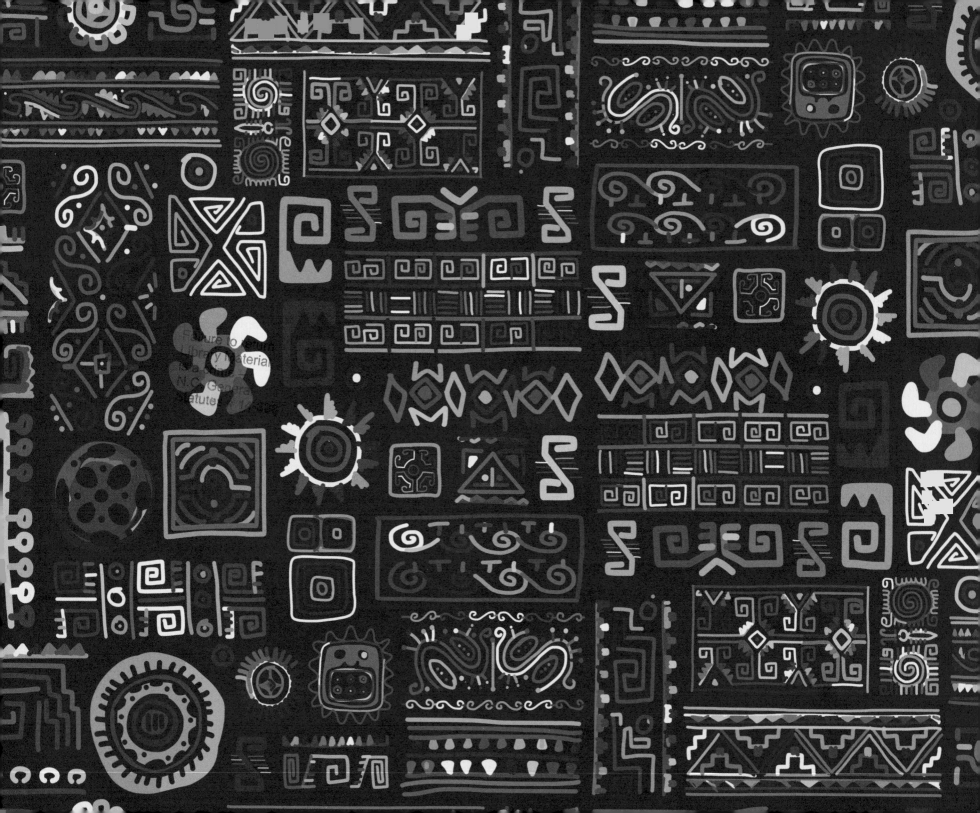